P9-EGM-683

ROSS DEAN
STRASSBURG LIBRARY
BOX 2
LIBRARY OF CONGRESS

EDGE BOOKS™

TRUE TALES OF SURVIVAL PRESENTS:

STRANDED IN THE SNOW!

ERIC LEMARQUE'S STORY OF SURVIVAL

by Tim O'Shei

Consultant:
Al Siebert, PhD
Author of *The Survivor Personality*

McLEAN-MERCER
REGIONAL LIBRARY
BOX 505
RIVERDALE, ND 58565

Capstone
press®
Mankato, Minnesota

Edge Books are published by Capstone Press,
151 Good Counsel Drive, P.O. Box 669, Mankato, Minnesota 56002.
www.capstonepress.com

Copyright © 2007 by Capstone Press. All rights reserved.
No part of this publication may be reproduced in whole or in part, or stored in a
retrieval system, or transmitted in any form or by any means, electronic, mechanical,
photocopying, recording, or otherwise, without written permission of the publisher.
For information regarding permission, write to Capstone Press,
151 Good Counsel Drive, P.O. Box 669, Dept. R, Mankato, Minnesota 56002.
Printed in the United States of America

Library of Congress Cataloging-in-Publication Data
O'Shei, Tim.
    Stranded in the snow!: Eric LeMarque's story of survival / by Tim O'Shei.
    p. cm.—(Edge books. True tales of survival)
    Summary: "Describes how snowboarder Eric LeMarque survived a week
stranded in the Sierra Nevada Mountains"—Provided by publisher.
    Includes bibliographical references and index.
    ISBN-13: 978-0-7368-6777-1 (hardcover)
    ISBN-10: 0-7368-6777-5 (hardcover)
    ISBN-13: 978-0-7368-7867-8 (softcover pbk.)
    ISBN-10: 0-7368-7867-X (softcover pbk.)
    1. Snowboarding—Sierra Nevada (Calif. and Nev.)—Anecdotes—Juvenile
literature. 2. Wilderness survival—Sierra Nevada (Calif. and Nev.)—Juvenile
literature. 3. LeMarque, Eric, 1969– —Juvenile literature. I. Title. II. Series.
GV857.S57O445 2007
796.93'9097944—dc22   2006024768

Editorial Credits
Angie Kaelberer, editor; Jason Knudson, designer; Wanda Winch, photo
    researcher/photo editor

Photo Credits
Corbis/Zandria Muench Beraldo, 6–7
Getty Images Inc./Photographer's Choice/Laurence Monneret, front cover, 26–27
Index Stock Imagery/James Kay, 24–25
Mammoth Mountain Ski Area, 4, 10, 11, 12–13, 16, 18–19, 22
Minden Pictures/Michael Quinton, 14–15
Peter Arnold/SIU, 21
Photo courtesy of Eric LeMarque, 27, 28, 29
Photodisc/Lee Cates, 1, 16–17 (background)
Shutterstock/Mag. Alban Egger, back cover; Mark Bonham, 22–23 (background);
    Mark E. Stout, 28–29 (background); mihaicalin, 4–5 (background), 32;
    Svetlana Larina, 2–3; TTphoto, 30–31
ZUMA Press/Davis Barber, 8

1 2 3 4 5 6 12 11 10 09 08 07

TABLE OF CONTENTS

ONE LAST RIDE

LEARN ABOUT:
- WINTER VACATION
- RIDING SOLO
- OUT OF BOUNDS

Eric spent several days snowboarding on Mammoth Mountain in California.

Eric noticed a path of fresh snow on the southeastern edge of the mountain.

The sky was darkening on the afternoon of February 6, 2004. Sunset was approaching.

Eric LeMarque and his friends had spent the week snowboarding on California's Mammoth Mountain. His friends left that morning, but Eric wasn't ready to make the trip home to Los Angeles. He wanted to coast down the 11,000-foot (3,350-meter) mountain one last time.

It was nearly 4 o'clock. That was closing time for Mammoth's ski and snowboard area. Eric noticed a path of fresh snow on the southeastern edge of the mountain. He steered his snowboard in that direction.

5

This area, called Dragon's Back, was out of bounds. People who snowboarded there had to find their own way back. There was no chairlift to haul riders up the mountain.

That didn't scare Eric, who loved adventure. He decided to ride down Dragon's Back. On his way down, he waved to a ski patroller.

Eric wouldn't wave to anyone else for a long time.

The Mammoth Mountain chairlift didn't reach where Eric planned to take his last run.

CHAPTER 2

LOST IN THE SNOW

8

Eric played both ice and in-line hockey in Los Angeles.

LEARN ABOUT:
- LIFELONG ATHLETE
- FACING THE DRAGON
- NO WAY OUT

Eric was born July 1, 1969, in Paris, France. Though his life started in Europe, Eric grew up in California. He excelled in sports as a kid. At Northern Michigan University, Eric was a star forward on the hockey team. In 1987, the Boston Bruins of the National Hockey League drafted him.

Although Eric never made it on an NHL roster, he played on the Bruins' minor league teams. He also played in Europe and on the French national team in the 1994 Winter Olympics.

After Eric stopped playing, he worked around Los Angeles as a hockey coach. Staying involved with the game helped him stay fit and healthy. So did his hobby of snowboarding. Eric loved the rush of speeding down a steep mountain.

Normally, Eric carried lots of safety gear when snowboarding. He packed spare clothes, a whistle, fruit, and protein bars. But for his February 6 ride, Eric figured he didn't need much equipment.

9

ONE MORE RIDE

Eric slept until noon on February 6. When he woke up, he snacked on some protein bars and headed to the mountain. His ski socks were soaked from the day before, so he didn't wear them. He didn't bring extra food or a safety whistle either. Because it was late in the day, Eric just wanted to do a couple of rides.

Signs guide snowboarders to the marked runs at Mammoth.

Mammoth Mountain is famous for its fresh powder.

Eric put on a T-shirt, long underwear, jacket, ski pants, regular socks, and a wool hat. His cell phone battery was dead, and he thought about stopping by a friend's place to recharge it. But he decided not to take the extra time.

At the resort, Eric took several long rides near the chairlift on the south end of the mountain. Then he found Dragon's Back. There was no chairlift, no markers—nothing to help anyone who got lost.

11

The sun was setting over the mountain by the time Eric realized he was lost.

EDGE FACT

Because of its location, Mammoth Mountain gets much more snow than the other Sierra Nevada peaks—an average of 400 inches (1,000 centimeters) each year.

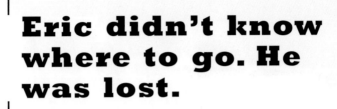

Eric didn't know where to go. He was lost.

Eric loved fresh powder and decided to be daring. He veered down the mountain, flowing fast and turning smoothly.

Finally, Eric came to a flat area. He stopped and decided to head back. He started walking in what he thought was the right direction. But an hour and a half later, he found himself back in the same spot. That's when Eric realized he was walking in circles.

Darkness was setting in. The temperature was freezing. Eric didn't know where to go. He was lost.

13

CHAPTER 3

BATTLING THE COLD

LEARN ABOUT:
- SURVIVING THE COLD
- INTO THE WILDERNESS
- RESCUE!

14

Eric chased away wild animals that may have been coyotes.

Eric was in trouble, but not too worried. He focused on surviving the night, figuring he'd find a road in the morning.

Eric sat down and took out his supplies. His cell phone battery was dead, but his MP3 player was working. He had no food, but he did have four pieces of gum. He had matches, but they were wet.

ANIMAL SCARE

For dinner, Eric chewed and swallowed two pieces of gum. For a fire, he gathered pine needles and ripped up bits of his hat and T-shirt. But his soggy matches wouldn't light.

That night, a small pack of hairy, doglike animals came near Eric. They appeared to be either wolves or coyotes. Eric screamed, scaring them away. He thought the smell of the gum might have attracted the animals, so he threw away the two remaining pieces.

After his scare, Eric wanted a weapon. He found a stick and used the edge of his snowboard to sharpen the ends. To protect himself from the cold wind, Eric dug a trench in the snow and slept in it.

Eric headed for the safety of Tamarack
Lodge, but he never made it there.

BAD DECISION

The next day, Eric saw the Mammoth Mountain ski lift far in the distance. To reach the ski lift, he would have to climb a steep slope. Instead, Eric decided to head for the nearby Tamarack Lodge resort.

That decision turned out to be a big mistake. Eric never found Tamarack Lodge. He kept going farther and farther into the Ansel Adams Wilderness. Eric's socks and boots were wet with snow in the bitter cold.

The Ansel Adams Wilderness covers 228,500 acres (92,500 hectares) in the Sierra and Inyo National Forests.

TOO CLOSE TO THE FALLS

Finally, Eric reached a river. He drank the water, which was safer than eating snow. Eating snow can cause the body's temperature to drop quickly. Eric walked on the river rocks, which was easier than trudging through the snow. But he slipped and fell into the river. The current almost pulled him over an 80-foot (24-meter) waterfall.

Eric made it out of the water, but he lost his left boot in the river. He took off his clothes and hung them on a tree to dry. Eric shivered as he used his snowboard to cut bark from trees. He ate some of the bark. He dug a hole in the snow for a bed and lined it with the rest of the bark for warmth.

EDGE FACT

Eric used the blue screen of his MP3 player to try to attract planes, but it was too small to be seen from the sky.

FROZEN FEET

During the next few days, Eric's physical condition became worse. His feet turned red, purple, and black from frostbite. When he took off his socks, the skin peeled off his feet. The rest of his body was covered in a rash from his clothing rubbing against his wet skin. He was quickly losing weight from eating only tree bark and pine nuts.

One night, Eric slept inside his jacket and almost choked from breathing his own carbon dioxide. People exhale carbon dioxide, but it's poisonous if breathed in large amounts. Eric had to open his jacket sleeves to let oxygen in.

Still, Eric's thinking was sharp. His MP3 player was equipped with a radio. The signal from a radio station near Mammoth became stronger when he pointed the player north. Eric headed in that direction. Using his snowboard as a pole, he slowly moved uphill. In some places, he was up to his chest in snow.

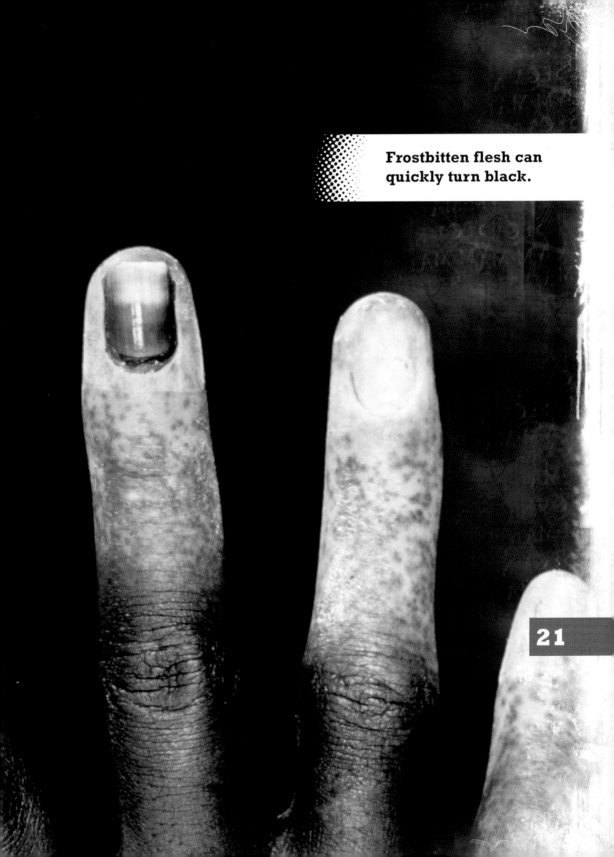

Frostbitten flesh can quickly turn black.

21

Ski patrollers were part of the group searching for Eric.

EDGE FACT

A lost skier, Chris Foley, had been discovered dead on Mammoth Mountain on February 1, 2004. He had been missing since January 6.

> # The patrollers figured the weather was just too harsh for anyone to survive.

WHERE'S ERIC?

Meanwhile, Eric's family was beginning to worry. On February 11, Eric's father, Philip, drove from Los Angeles to Mammoth Mountain. No one there had seen Eric for five days. Philip called the police, and rescuers sprang into action. The sheriff's search-and-rescue team scouted by snowmobile. Ski patrollers looked for any sign of Eric.

For two days, they found nothing. But on the morning of February 13, a group of ski patrollers found a trail. They followed it south, down the mountain and into the wilderness. Along the way, they found Eric's shredded clothing and his snowboard tracks. They believed Eric was dead. The patrollers figured the weather was just too harsh for anyone to survive.

23

A rescue helicopter searched the ground and trees below.

24

After 9 miles (14 kilometers), the ski patrol was called back. Rescuers began searching for Eric by helicopter. The timing was good, because Eric was reaching high ground. With his right foot in a boot and the left one bare, Eric was mostly crawling. He had traveled 14 miles (23 kilometers) from the Mammoth ski resort. He knew if no one found him, he would soon be dead.

FOUND!

When Eric saw a helicopter fly overhead, he yelled as loud as he could. The people in the helicopter saw Eric and told rescuers on the ground where to find him. The date was Friday, February 13, 2004—one week after Eric first coasted down Dragon's Back.

When rescuers reached Eric, he told them that he wanted to get into a hot tub. Instead, they took him to a hospital.

CHAPTER 4

THE LONG ROAD BACK

LEARN ABOUT:

- CLOSE CALL
- AMAZING RECOVERY
- A NEW LIFE

Hockey great Wayne Gretzky visited Eric in the hospital.

Eric was in bad shape. He was dehydrated from lack of liquids. He had lost 35 pounds (16 kilograms). His body temperature was only 88 degrees Fahrenheit (31 degrees Celsius). Normal body temperature is 98.6 degrees Fahrenheit (37 degrees Celsius).

Eric also had severe frostbite in his feet. The water in his cells had frozen. Muscle, blood, and tissue cells had burst. Gangrene had set in. Left untreated, this rotting infection would spread to the rest of his body. Doctors had to amputate both of his feet. Later, they amputated another 6 inches (15 centimeters) of his legs.

The situation could have been worse. One of the rescuers said that Eric would not have survived another night in the mountains. His doctors agreed it was a miracle he was alive.

Eric now plays hockey using his prosthetic legs.

DANGEROUS ADVENTURE

The story of Eric's amazing survival got lots of attention. Eric said that during his ordeal, he tried to keep calm. But he admitted that by the last day, he was frightened.

After his surgery, doctors fitted Eric with artificial legs. He spent six months learning how to walk again. In 2005, he played for the U.S. Paralympic hockey team. Best of all, he is snowboarding again.

Eric LeMarque loves wild rides, and he isn't ready to give them up.

Eric lives in California with his wife, Hope, and their son, Nicholas.

29

GLOSSARY

amputate (AM-pyuh-tate)—to cut off someone's arm, leg, or other body part, usually because the part is damaged

carbon dioxide (KAR-buhn dye-OK-side)—a gas that people exhale; carbon dioxide can kill people if they breathe in too much of it.

coyote (KYE-oht)—a wolflike animal that lives throughout much of the United States

dehydration (dee-hye-DRAY-shuhn)—a health condition caused by lack of water

frostbite (FRAWST-bite)—a condition that occurs when cold temperatures freeze skin

gangrene (GANG-green)—a condition that occurs when flesh decays

Paralympics (pa-ruh-LIM-piks)—a series of international competitions for athletes with disabilities

READ MORE

Doeden, Matt. *Snowboarding.* To the Extreme. Mankato, Minn.: Capstone Press, 2005.

Markle, Sandra. *Rescues!* Minneapolis: Millbrook, 2006.

O'Shei, Tim. *The World's Most Amazing Survival Stories.* The World's Top 10s. Mankato, Minn.: Capstone Press, 2007.

INTERNET SITES

FactHound offers a safe, fun way to find Internet sites related to this book. All of the sites on FactHound have been researched by our staff.

Here's how:

1. Visit *www.facthound.com*

2. Choose your grade level.

3. Type in this book ID **0736867775** for age-appropriate sites. You may also browse subjects by clicking on letters, or by clicking on pictures and words.

4. Click on the **Fetch It** button.

FactHound will fetch the best sites for you!

INDEX